RUGRATS in Paris THE MOVIE

A Dream Come True!

Adapted by Donna Taylor
Based on the Script by
David N. Weiss & J. David Stem
and Jill Gorey & Barbara Herndon
and Kate Boutilier

Illustrated by Vince Giarrano

Simon Spotlight/Nickelodeon

New York   London   Toronto   Sydney   Singapore

KLASKY CSUPO INC.

Based on the TV series *Rugrats*® created by Arlene Klasky, Gabor Csupo, and Paul Germain as seen on Nickelodeon®

SIMON SPOTLIGHT
An imprint of Simon & Schuster Children's Publishing Division
1230 Avenue of the Americas
New York, New York 10020

Copyright © 2000 Paramount Pictures and Viacom International Inc.
All rights reserved. NICKELODEON, *Rugrats*, and all related titles, logos, and characters
are trademarks of Viacom International Inc.

All rights reserved including the right of
reproduction in whole or in part in any form.

SIMON SPOTLIGHT and colophon are registered trademarks of Simon & Schuster.

Manufactured in the United States of America

First Edition

2 4 6 8 10 9 7 5 3 1

ISBN 0-689-83336-9

Everyone was excited! They were going to Paris, France. Tommy's dad, Stu, had been asked to fix a Reptar he had designed for Reptarland there.

When they arrived, Stu and Chas, Chuckie's dad, took Angelica and the babies to Reptarland.

"Welcome," greeted a smiling woman named Kira.

"I'm Stu," said Stu, "and this is my good friend, Charles Finster."

"Call me Chas," said Chas. "And this is my son, Chuckie."

"Hi, Chuckie," said Kira. "Oh, what a nice bear!"
Then Angelica introduced the babies. "The bald
one's Tommy and that's his drooly brother Dil and
the gross ones are Phil and Lil and I'm Angelique
and I speak French! Parsley-voo fran-cy?"

Kira laughed and said, "Oui, yes!"

While the grown-ups were talking, the babies found a gigantic Reptar head—and the mean-spirited Coco LaBouche! Coco was Kira's boss. She did not like children.

"What are those filthy bookends doing here?" she shouted, pointing at the babies. "Call the dogcatcher, the exterminator . . . do something, Jean-Claude!"

Kira and Chas decided to take the
babies to the Princess Parade.
The parade was wonderful!

"The princess is coming!" said Kira. "Let me tell you her story." Kira explained that Reptar once lived in a village, but the people were afraid of him and chased him into the forest.

"There he met a beautiful princess who recognized how kindhearted and lonely he was. She promised to take care of him and keep him safe forever and ever."

Chuckie couldn't take his eyes off the princess. He wanted her for his mom. She would surely take care of him forever!

That evening Kira brought her daughter, Kimi, to meet everyone.

"Please come to the park with us tomorrow," Chas said to Kimi.

Suddenly Coco said, "I'll join you."

No one knew that Coco had a plan to marry someone so that she could be the boss of Reptarland. And Coco had decided that she would marry Chas even though she didn't like him!

Meanwhile the babies and Kimi were getting along just fine.

"Do you live in Reptarland?" Tommy asked.

"No," answered Kimi, "but since my mom works here, I get to come all the time."

"Do you know the princess?" asked Chuckie.

"Uh, no," said Kimi, "but I know she lives in a castle on that bowlcano."

The next day Coco and Chas took the kids on the Ooey-gooey Ride. Coco was not having any fun!

In the distance Tommy spotted the princess's castle. "Let's go see the princess," he said.

"We can't," said Chuckie. "This ride is moving!"

That didn't matter to Kimi. She crawled along the railing, and Chuckie and the babies soon followed.

When Coco discovered that the babies were missing, she didn't tell Chas. Instead she called for the special Ninja security guards. The babies didn't know that Ninja guards were after them. They were too busy looking for the princess's castle.

Finally Kimi led her friends to the volcano. "I told ya
I knowed the short cup!"

The princess stood at the castle door and waved. Chuckie
toddled toward her, just as she turned to go back into the castle.

"Oh, no!" moaned Chuckie. "She's gone!"

"She's right inside," said Tommy. "Go in!"

As Chuckie approached the front door, an enormous, fierce-looking dragon glared at him. He began to back away.

Suddenly the security guards grabbed Chuckie and the other babies and returned them to Coco and Chas.

"I didn't get to meet the princess," said Chuckie. "I wish I wasn't such a scaredy-cat!"

That night Chuckie dreamed that he was about to open the door to the princess's castle. But there was that mean-looking dragon!
"H-H-Hello? Where am I?" he asked.

And then scary warriors surrounded him. They looked even meaner!
"Aaahhh!" cried Chuckie.

Suddenly Chuckie turned into a fearless fighter.
And the dragon stood, big and fierce, in front of him.
"Grr . . ." the scowling creature growled.
But Chuckie bravely grabbed the dragon
and flipped him over his shoulder! Then he
triumphantly kicked open the castle door!

It was just a dream, but when Chuckie woke up, he still felt good inside. "Guess what, Tommy," he said. "I dreamed I was real brave. I'm ready to meet the princess!"

"That's great, Chuckeroo!" said Tommy. "'Cause we're gonna see the princess at the Reptar show today."

At the show Chuckie was thrilled to see the princess onstage. He couldn't wait to give his teddy bear to the princess and tell her how happy he would be to have her as his mother.

Chuckie held the bear out toward the princess. As she reached for it, he gasped. The princess behind the fan was really Coco!

And worst yet, Chas later announced that he was planning to *marry* Coco!

Chuckie was so unhappy. Tears ran down his cheeks as he told his friends, "I want a mommy who smiles and talks nice to me and tucks me in at night and tells me stories . . . a mommy who really loves me."

Then suddenly he cried out, "We gots to stop the wedding!"

Coco was so mean that on her wedding day she asked her assistant, Jean-Claude, to hide the babies until the ceremony was over.

But the babies had a plan of their own. First, Angelica tied up Jean-Claude. Then, with Chuckie at the controls, the babies fled in the Reptar that Stu had fixed.

Meanwhile Jean-Claude had untied himself and was on the loose! He was riding Robosnail . . . right toward Reptar!

Chuckie was braver than ever. He fought off Robosnail and forced it into the volcano! Then he and the babies hurried to the church.

"NOOO!" yelled Chuckie as they ran inside. Chas finally got the message and stopped the wedding.

But, to Chuckie's delight, six months later Chas married . . .

Kira. Chuckie finally got a mom—and a sister, too! Chuckie's dream had really come true!